Splintered & Splintering

Poetry

Gregory D. Strawn

Splinters
Splintered & Splintering

Gregory D. Strawn

§

A Scorched Sand Silhouette
Roseville, California

"I will multiply thy seed . . . as the *sand*
which is upon the sea shore . . .
I have refined thee . . . in the *furnace*
of affliction"

(Genesis 22:17 & Isaiah 48:10).

Indeed,
I was cut
often—and from time to time,
deep—

For

My Grandchildren:

Jackson MacKay Krebs
Brooklyn Christine Krebs
Calin Warren Kai Eshbaugh
Isla Korina Strawn
Theron Robert Ryo Eshbaugh
Eva Beverly Strawn
Brayden William Krebs
Patrick Kelly Strawn
Alora Louise Strawn
Owen MacKay Strawn
Ada Denise Strawn
Shane O'Connor Strawn

and
All Others Yet Unborn

Forward

Most things existing here in mortality, mundane or magnificent, essential or trivial, silent or raucous—eventually brake, and some of the more fragile and *dramatic* of these varied finite things actually shatter, splinter, scatter, and sometimes even *squeal* in their dispersion. Regardless of the mode of fracturing, the shrapnel of devastation within each such circumstance is clearly manifest in the resulting variances in visages, weights, and sounds within each fragmented thing—manifesting within themselves as striking complexities of piercing, vital forms—and every single shard of these splinterings is cuttingly sharp, as is the natural motif of even the most ordinary of broken, fractured, and shattered things. In many, if not most, circumstances, those things that are *splintered* are actually still *splintering*—in that they continue to fragment—sometimes, it seems, almost indefinitely. In kind, the splintered as well as the splintering shards become, in their devolution, very minute, almost infinitesimal—still, they remain piercing. I have discovered that the smaller the prick, the more intense the referendum of its pain.

I have also uncovered this clever key to navigating the sharp, powerful, painful, and essential aspects of mortality, as well as interacting compassionately with humanity at its most fragile and tender level. It requires learning to *purposefully* walk and live and laugh and cry within the delicate, continuously splintering fragments, managing both the splinters as well as the wounds that they inevitably will inflict— patiently, looking always to God for calming clarity and redeeming respite. While it is not reasonable, nor is it even desirable, to altogether avoid the piercing and the cutting—and even the pain, making all of the blood spilt in the process worth the corresponding sacrifice is powerful medicine to the *spirit that shrieks* within the broken things themselves— as well as a healing salve, that reaches deep within the *heaviest of the hearts* of the breakers of things, no matter the breadth or the depth of the inevitable scattering and piercing of conscience. And there really can be peace for both the breaker and the broken—because open wounds; pierced, rattled, and shattered minds; as well as sunken, shrieking, and withered hearts will heal—they certainly will all be healed. Even spilt blood regenerates with time.

And I am also a *thing* that has broken and shattered and fragmented and healed and even regenerated—over and over throughout my time in mortality. I have concurrently owned the heavy Heart of a breaker of things as well as the splintered Spirit of one who has been broken. I have received and I have given wounds. I forgave, and I have been forgiven. I have been bold, and I have been skittish. I am a man who is often, still, a small, frightened, little boy. During my iterations as this child, I have from time to time failed in my fidelity to manhood. I have also labored under many seasons of honor and joy and peace. As a man, I have at times fragmented my memory from what was still essential to retain from my childhood in my attempt to become a *truer* man. I am a miracle; I am a curse. I am a melancholic optimist, both mourning and rejoicing in turn, according to the juxtaposition of the seasons aligned for and against my conscience. I have loved so powerfully that I have forgotten to breathe. At times, I have forgotten to love and have, inadvertently, passed up the enviable suffocation of passion. I have both laughed-and-enjoyed and suffered-and-cried, perhaps more than even the average child; I have lost much of my childlike laughter to serious reflection in adulthood. I have rocked to the rebellious music of my generation; I have swayed and I have danced—and I did love it. I have fought within, throughout, and beyond so much personal suffering as I have worshipped through the proprietary musical cannons of faith and prayer. I have sat by myself—left out of the joy. I have been the life of the party as well as the death of enjoyable conversation. I have been a passionate teacher of truths and a reticent student of realities. I have slept outside in the daylight; I have remained awake all night. I have been full of health and vigor, and I have been frail and weak.

In essence, I have been a singularity: an ordinary human-being.

After Things Shatter

I. The Abode of the Newly Broken

II. The Random Shards that Pierce and Cut

III. Finding and Collecting the Pieces

IV. The Mosaic

V. The Cure for All Wounds

Dedicated to My Brother

Kirtis Jay Strawn

1959-2018

Thank you for Surfing and Skating with me.
I miss you. I love you.

I bled no more than other poets . . .

Splinters of Rose

The death of even a single rose
within a cloistered cluster
is itself a serious matter for poetic minds—
but yesterday
as I sat writing this very poem,
I could feel solitary, single stems
bright bunches and bouquets
and even entire grandiose gardens
fading pale,
drooping before dropping—
then shattering
as tint-crystal *Splinters*
in cubistic patterns
across the frigid floor of my mind.

I continued to compose,
carefully arranging that chaos of fragments into artful words
before massaging them into metaphors and symbols and motifs
with the soft flesh of my forefinger.

Indeed,
I was cut
often—and from time to time
deep—

yet I bled no more than other poets
who, upon seeing bright roses braking,
understand, that despite the pain,
they have no other reasonable recourse
than to minister among the *Splinters*.

Elsewhere is the Where I belong . . .

I.

The Abode
of the Newly Broken

Elsewhere

I have become pale—for
I am worn ever so thin
in this:
    my belief
that Elsewhere is the Where *I* belong—
for Nowhere never *did* exist, and
Somewhere is obnoxiously overcrowded,
    overrated, and—of course—
so very tedious.

Still—

Elsewhere is the very Where I can never
    confront,
for when I am approaching—
snorting powerfully near its portal,
it tactlessly transforms to Hereabouts
or the Here where I already reside, and
alas—Elsewhere is once again
    diminutive—

even vaporous

ever beyond
my reach.

FINDING THE POET

There is something between us,
just sitting there, fossilized -- fixed --
a fence, a field, a country, a continent,
    a world, a universe,
and it parts us
as two leaves of hair
    cut by the bars of a comb,
and I am whisked to poetry
and you are searching,
searching (though you know it not) for a poet.

I, as a poet, need to be found
and understood and parted
like an ocean sliced by the wake
    of a dolphin or shark or minnow or whale,
    gliding equal to the lines of my swellings,
not by a ship, nor any vessel, intruder
    pounding my ripples smooth
    denying my right to be the rise that I am.
Only creatures residing within the confines
    of my optical sea can be partakers
    of the gifts in me, --
and it must be someone,
someone searching across fences and continents,
    fields and universes,
    breaking bars, leaving the hoary head
    as a single mass of meshed, matted hair.

And I see that something between you and me.
It is clear and bound as the product of a poets pen.
The ancient form is cracking. Look. See.
I must preserve it, memorialize it,
    place it in a museum, an ocean, imensity of space.
But it will take both you and me to move
    reality to its place.
Keep searching, my friend.
I am old and will become older still
    with the parting of days
and someday all things will shuffle
    into the proper perspective of what was and what is,
and the sea will deepen
and the universe will thin
and the poet will be found
by the reader, searching in the poem.
immersed within his poem.

The Scribbler

There is clear—yet creatively concealed—reason
in the ornate sub-scratchings
which adorn so many of the pages
within the many folios that I own:
    notebooks, textbooks, magazines,
    calendars, novels, treatises, biographies,
    holy writ, reference texts, dictionaries,
    and anthologies.

You may perceive it as I believe it—
it is persistently there

inside that cross-hatched, spectral dungeon
wherein waits the forlorn, feminine figure—
gilded resignation, dim
behind that dense prison door:
Hester, content in her confinement[1]—
Indeed, she is no less representative of truth than what Picasso
might have cogently composed
had he been there,
so long-far away—

as was I.

You may sense it when I commence it—
it is certainly clear

when my eyes retrace these circular 'esses'
up the aboriginal Congo
reticently trailing Marlow,
stifled and stymied in his *darkest* journey[2]—

---

[1] Reference to Hester Prynne in Nathanial Hawthorne's novel, *The Scarlet Letter*
[2] Reference to Marlow in Joseph Conrad's novel, *Heart of Darkness*

as have I.

You may comprehend it as I understand it—
it is defiantly here

periodically punctuated by these dots,
descending in digit-like drips
above *Black's*
legal analysis of "delinquency."[3]
Those belligerent, bellicose
youths could never explain the discontent
central to themselves
with greater accuracy
than in these several marks
have I.

You may ever heed it as I have seen it—
it is powerfully near,

displayed in these boxes
stacked impossibly edge-to-edge,
stair-step both above and below
John's *Revelation*,[4]
and the journey of *Everyman*
as *he* nears the end of all the world[5]—
either up-step through the boxes
or descending head-first-down.

It remains indelible:

a fierce reality—an ongoing remonstrance—

---

[3] Reference to *Black's Legal Dictionary*
[4] Reference to the New Testament, Book of Revelations
[5] Reference to the English Morality Play, *The Summoning of Everyman*, written in the 1400s
AD

Or perhaps, a powerful acceptance—
heretofore chased down, left alone,
    sought after, hidden away deep, learned from,
and—for you and for me—from now
until ever after

deliberately found.

. . . imagining turbulence
when there *is* only peace—

The Slip—The Slide

In this, our present and fragile sphere of *time*,
    inevitably
all things will compress and expand, fracture, splinter, and then slip
    downhill,
on occasion, even forcibly folding into themselves
ribbon-candy-like—and at other times
clotting, expanding, and building
    bulbous
amassing as mountainous wavering
    wads,
only to slide

down, down—

tumbling and stumbling over their own
misunderstood, unforgiving, and calloused
    slopes,
oozing into the *depressions* of valleys
seeping into the *anxieties* of caverns
until they fill completely—and then slowly
    spill
beyond their overburdened brims,
bulging and undulating, haltingly forward,
passively lurching ever
    shoreward
until they lose themselves within the *manic*
depths of the unfathomable
seas—slipping, as it were,
    unnoticed

down, down—

    for millennia

down—

melding magmatic into the reticent
rip of continents,

pressing intently
    passionately
        although silently

down, down—

into the *captivating* core
of the earth.

Median

Sometimes,
early in the morning
during the clearest hours of consciousness
when intellect opposes me for spite
    (or, perhaps, primeval reflex)
I wish I were merely

Median—

not obtuse, not extreme in any way—
simply middle-of-the-road, average

Calm—

but *this* fledgling Walleye is already
gelatinous,
ripped, bleeding, disfigured—
and I have hardly even begun the swim
upstream—

Have just been existing here
    abiding
tight in my nature—
a habitat for friction, fiction, and fear: the extreme
    antediluvian
evolving oceans away from that enviable

Median

of which Aristotle and Gotama spoke.

And I have grown
as distinct as the splintered stone-scape
distinguishing the Alleghenies from its mother Appalachians

yet as vague as the nostalgia seeping in and about
all wavering, deep green
    grasses,
brilliant, emerald-blue ocean
    plains,
and even my childhood's cold, concrete
    waves—
        solid, yet fluid—firm, yet somehow undulating
        with disingenuous visions of becoming
Centered, ever Moderate—
Mean

Once again, Calm—

That Someone Else who I often
imagine might become me,
    eventually
because it is Good,
it is Right—yet
I never was, never have been—
    seemingly
never would be,

in life's reality, in *my* actuality,
I never am—

and then, hesitant within this haze, my primeval brain
clicks half past
    hope

as I all too often shred myself, mercilessly,
on the soft, sandy shoals,
reflexively, violently, impossibly—
imagining Turbulence
when there *is* only Peace—
ripping myself from clear

Median

because my nature, in which I persist,
beguiles me to pull painfully,
tirelessly, even forcefully
away—to strain hard, at all costs,
tearing myself apart—
even when I fully understand
that it is my own flesh
I am pulling from off
my own tried and tired bones.

As my heart—opened and exposed—
sags beneath and drags below
me, I will still obstinately persist to pull
apart from clear

Median,

and—in this vulnerable state—my
heart is often pierced
by sharp rocks and discarded debris
hidden low, beneath the raucous rapids—
Still, somehow, I do not recognize it at all.

*   *   *

In truth—
I really do desire this illusive

Median

in the same way
a career politician or a long-term Head of State
wants to be *nobody*

once again—
even while campaigning
for another term in office.

Eleanor Rigby?[6]
Her regular routine is a mere pipedream
    for me.

I will not partake of her smoke.
Instead, I submit to lesser
castes of fear.

Median

seems unattainable by my tier,
restrained within the extremes—my habitat:

    erosion of mind
    implosion of heart
    expulsion of soul.

Still, I swim on—
hoping and believing
that I will, in fact, come to an *absolute*
understanding that somewhere, sometime,
    somehow,
there will appear a panaceaic net
which will safely catch me
and save me from the drowning justice
of remaining permanently, everlastingly

me.

---

[6] Reference to the song "Eleanor Rigby," 1966, by the Beatles

... the possibility of peace
someday—

Patience

My Soul—please
have patience with me
    today—

I have had so very little
patience for the man writing this poem
for over sixty
    years—

a long time—yet I really do know him, and I perceive
that, at some very real level, he
is also a legitimate human being
    even now—

It is also true that all people
desire to be viewed with patience and compassion
    always—

so, because of this, there ever looms
the possibility of hope, of grace, of peace
    someday—

for him—for *me*—for you, also—for all of those
other people we do not even know
who plead for relief within their Souls—
    today.

It Wants

I am terribly troubled within this wan
world
I have chosen to inhabit.

It wants
stimulus, not substance,
and it stimulates itself beyond
numbness.

It wants
tentative *justice*, not kindness, and it adjudicates
partisan treason and terror—
softly.

    Bigoted and "past feeling,"
    it murders
    mercy.

It wants
Leisure, not honor,
and it "lies in wait" to take its clear
advantage.

It wants
Appearance, not integrity,
and it defiles the simple and exterminates
the meek.

It wants
Filth, not chastity,
and it opens that which is sacred to perversion
and abuse.

It wants.

It takes—

It wants.
It destroys—

It wants
you.

It wants
me.

. . . I tend to wax silent—

The Question

I do not own
the answer
as do so many *brilliant*
others:

>the ignorant
>the tactless
>the vindictive
>the asinine—

who fiercely whip me for my upstart
pseudo-normalcy with their caste-
of-no-tales
devoured in the faux history
of the *Plebeians* and the *Proles*
who are neverywhere present,

all the while brooding
belligerent in their cyclical
redundancies,

and even then,
I tend to wax silent—
ever embracing my Socratic
emptiness,
rejecting what is commonly asserted

in favor of the nucleo-genesis of the answer:

the question.

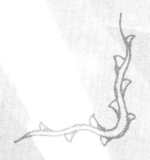

II.

The Random Shards
That Pierce and Cut

There Has Always Been *Someone*

There has always been
Someone
walking so deliberately
sometimes, even desperately
behind me—

following me.

When I was a young child, *it* was the adult
    son of the high school history teacher
        who lived down the hill and across the street,
    who also thought it prudent to there inter
        his dead dog's sawdust-filled carcass—and entreat it,
        commission it, to snarl with an ethereal glare
    as a glass-eyed, faux, demi-dog trophy, elite
        guardian of his home and hearth—forever
    wreathed in wasabi and wild mustard
        bamboo.

This *man,* my neighbor's son, regularly remained
        as latent, living, human statuary
secreted within the foliage, which wildly framed
        his recessed and darkened driveway—

domestic tableau:

Man Waits in Driveway for Children to Stalk—

until my classmates and I
daily passed by.

He would then follow us, lurching

haltingly in his labor—still, he would always retreat,
   uncomfortably, at the nether boundaries of his property's
   passive demarcation, whereat unfulfilled and in defeat
he would reluctantly drift aft, head held down to shield his eyes,
   retracing his heavy, awkward steps, in gawky rewind—
   stumbling back to his familiar driveway staging area
   once again, fading invisible into the lush and leafy blind

where *he* would simply wait—clunky, inert, and blank-faced—
   for the next naive child's passing. While in the meantime,
   for what seemed like ages, silent and still—he posed—in place.

Other children
like clockwork
always came—

These stalkings of statuary and traumas from trophy . . .

   They followed me.
   They beleaguered me.
   They threatened me.

As a pre-teen, *it* was doubt, unnatural sensitivity,
and if I am to be perfectly
honest—
fear
that stalked me

always right there, awkwardly
behind me—

ever near, pretentious yet aware
so abrasive, coarse, and constantly severe—
reproving, incessantly remanding,
unflinchingly reminding
me—

that I was *not* that
which I *should* have been,
which I *could* have been—

Beleaguered beneath the seasoned shadows of my father,
passively pursued by his depth: fathoms of artistic
eloquence—leagues of incomparable, picturesque
perfection, always there, quietly dignified and ever
glorious—
never me

Beleaguered outside the impossible boundaries of my brother,
sequestered without his recursive realms of innovative
individuality—regions of enthralling art, always another
ocean and more concrete to master—continually creative,
full of speed and skill and form—ever
beyond me

and therein and there-out and thereby,
I perpetually followed after all of my most oblique

fears—retracting back within the shadows,
waiting in the wings, constantly questioning my weak
efforts to become . . .

They followed me.
They beleaguered me.
They threatened me.

As an adult, it is the transient trophy
of reputation and the granite, habitual
status-seeking which leads to woke statuary—
coaxing while urging the oafishly tall
follower of convention to exit the clammy
covert of shadows and accost and trouble
me in my passing—

These, along with my heightening
angst
under-arching my most quieting,
ineloquent
even artless habitudes of hyperbole
and my nervous, near-earnest
efforts—to *be* . . .

are all still haltingly
staged—

> He who now accosts me, so tirelessly,
> so painstakingly, is at present—

> *Me*

> a strange, wan, and awkward man
> retracing, rewinding, returning—interred
> within those deep shadows, again—

> Yet I am not at all surprised
> within this acute, defining revelation,
> in this knowledge actualized—

For Now and for Then—
Even for Always—
this man,

this Me—

> *He* follows me.
> *He* beleaguers me.
> *He* threatens me.

. . . and I was frail, failing, nearly falling to the snow—

Ignorance

Ignorance is huge,
often as obvious
as a large abscess
from lip to eye—
oozing.

Still,
trapped within this folly,
a man will often claim soundness
of face and of body—
even as maggots
surge forth.

Ignorance is not kind
to the host. It consumes all
that could have been
beautiful and free—
festering, breeding,
becoming by default:

    Preferred Prejudice
    Intellectual Deformity
    Sneering Hatred
    Seeded Certitude

Manipulation of *fact*—

Manufactured *truth*.

I Fear: Part I

I do not know much for certain,
    and I have a fierce *trepidation*
of all that will remain
    unknown.

    I *fear* above all
that I might succeed
when justice would have me
    fail.

I *fear* kindness and warmth.
I *fear* love that would bind me—
    security and peace.

I *fear*. I *fear*. I tremble in *fear*

    of happiness.

Old Man

As the prowling pack of disheveled youths trudge,
swaggering while stampeding down the hall,
I watch, questioning and wondering how . . .

"What-cha' lookin' at, old man,"
one of them sneers as he passes by.
The others, although silent, join
the obligatory, wolf pack stare down—and I

look behind me—there is no one—
Then glance from side to side—still, no one.
I am the lone
adult—

—"Old Man."

And—unexpectedly, I am
transported back in time—
two decades.

There was another youth,
another question in search of truth

—same me.

In response to his tirade about "all of the old
people" holding him back and "keeping him
down," foolishly, I asked that boy, still in control,
"When you say, 'old' to whom do you refer?"

He wheeled around in his chair, pointing
directly at me, and in an angry, snarling
growl, he quickly retorted

—"You!"

That was the first time, in fact,
that I had ever consciously considered
the plausibility of the physiological prospect
that, perhaps,

I *was* "old."

I was suddenly the feeble man in Pyle's, "Salem Wolf."[7]
It was cold, and I was frail, failing, nearly
falling to the snow—I'd had enough—
the taunting wolf, panting sideways, eerily
glaring, patiently waiting for me,
decrepit in heart and mind,
to collapse—at least to drop upon my knees.

That was many years ago.

Presently,
as the alpha leads his pack
toward the restroom, there is no doubt—
I am, in fact,

"old—"

but I will not fall, will not cower back—
nor will I become the victim,
the prey of his attack.

Still—it jars me
internally,
when the words come verbally

---

[7] Reference to artwork by Howard Pyle for his story, "The Salem Wolf," published in Harper's Magazine, December 1909.

so blatantly
caustic.

Yes, they address me point-blank,

and hit me
precisely
between my eyes.

I Fear: Part II

There are times when I fear
    these words:

        Thou shalt "not enter in . . ."[8]
        "I know you not . . .
        Depart from me . . ."[9]

    formidable diction—

For I have longed for—with a dusty desire—

    goodness,

yet I have frequently faltered
throughout the lengthy living of my life.

    And

the sun's recline
    ever
marks my time,
notching the dry earth
    deep
with shadows of my name.

Therein dwells my fear—that
    I will age:
        not like wine
        not like cheese—but

like warm fish.

---

[8] From the New Testament, Hebrews 3:18
[9] From the New Testament, Matthew 7:23

I only grasp fingerfuls of
air.

You

I can no longer understand
    you.

I, therefore, do not recognize
    you—

even as I sit here for hours
    staring into the pale visage
    always fixed in place before me
    which somehow almost resembles
you—

for underneath that clay facade,
    an interloper, imposter dwells—
    pressure-forged by years of doubts
    and years of fears—all replacing
you—

and every time I reach after
    you,

I only grasp fingerfuls of
    air.

Night

There are *exactly* ten truths
carrying the night
which recurrently entrap me—ten
often underappreciated verities
retaining the evening,
and it is now my obligation
to enumerate *three* of them.
> (The others will remain hidden—incognito—
> for centuries, for all I care. Explaining these
> others is *not* my task.)

So—here it goes:

Number One: It is dark.
Number Two: Dark is stifling.
Number Three: All Stifling will soon be over.

And—I am bound to these.
They inform my very core. Still,
I must rise in my might
despite *all* realities

and choose . . . the light—

Then—this night,
its dank truth, will evolve and become
what it never was intended to be—

for the sun will truly

    rise again
        and again—

        and again.

Paper Idols

You are beaten—

By the reticent residue of your recalcitrant past,
you are slain.

You have given up on what might actually heal,
for you have enlisted *wholly resentment*
as your Constant Companion
and have made *selfishness*
your Still Small Voice,
permitting it to terrorize your mind with the re-
sharpened shrapnel of that singular
miserable memory:

some tangible yet transitory creation of your psyche—
a herd of gilded, papier mâché calves,[10]
even a multi-theistic, self-deprecating
worship of Fear
along with all her Stern, unrelenting Sisters:

    Resentment
    Self-Pity
    Rage
    Rationalization
    Revenge

And you—
all the while
are kneeling on the moist banks of the Fountain of Living
Water,
watching on, as your fragile Idols

---

[10] A reference to the golden calf that Aaron made for Israel when Moses was in the mount, receiving the ten commandments (Exodus 32)

dissipate
in His cleansing current—

yet you continue frantically,
fruitlessly in your attempts to Redeem them—
heaping up their soggy and disintegrating
gilded Paper carcasses
as Grotesque mounds of crude, disfigured
hopelessness upon the face of the
earth—

All the while
ignoring the waiting water which *will*
heal you, a painfully near arm's reach away.

Instead, you cry into the coarse sand,
prostrate before the soggy, limp, humanistic
mounds created by your own
trembling hands,
as you retch in agony
over what "might have been"
rather than looking forward
to the Day that *will* come
with wings saturated in Gilead's
Balm[11]—

Understanding
Forgiveness
Peace
Love

and Eternal Hope.

---

[11] An ancient and rare perfume, also used as a medicine

All the while
ignoring the water which might
heal you

Chewing Gum

If I was this wad
of used chewing gum,
I could be hidden easily
in out of the way places
(under tabletops,
on chair legs, even
at the bottom
of old tin trashcans).

Unfortunately for you,
I'm a man.

It's not so easy
to hide me
when you're tired of me,
or to force my disappearance
when your conversation with me
is finished—
and I
continue on and on.

Dearth of Reality

The hot breath, escaping the Body of truth
sears itself forcibly into my hardened flesh—
conviction by continued discussion—exacerbation
in and throughout so many deep, darkened
rooms within those most secluded of all secret
places—spaces wherein the ancient Gadiantons
gasp and combine their breaths into oral stealth[12]—
as covert emissaries, possessing modern, blood-filled
corpses which wittingly strut without and about—
before sneering within the mingling of their minds,
leering maliciously upon the many entrapped innocent
others, speaking *their* truths to the weak. Thereafter,
once so powerful and eternally immutable—Poetic

Truth—

becomes cleverly, callously, and creatively dismissed,
misperceived and ignored, even as it is denounced—
while its Fiction is fully embraced, paraded about,
honored and solemnly recognized before becoming
canonized as the answer which is the cancer that
engenders heartache and deflowers innocence—Then
that innocence stumbles regressive over the barren
landscape—gasps for oxygen, reaches out a slight,
trembling hand. Begging for sustenance, it calls
silently for assistance through dry and parched
lips, waits small in darkness, while that darkness
only deepens—collapsing memories and worlds
and hope into *Knowledge*; then that innocence

Dies.

---

[12] Reference to the Gadianton Robbers, a secret criminal organization, about 52 BC (Helaman 1:11)

Deceit

Time argues tirelessly against deceit.
It chisels deep and indelible canyons,
peerless yet irregular petroglyphs
upon its ever-aging facial cliffs—
carefully cataloguing the atrocities,
the choices, the secret pasts,
the injustices, the hidden pain—

And the tears that follow *what-ifs*
only tend to deepen channels, widen
gaps between flesh and flesh-
and-bone, until only the slightest
sullen glance dashes the visage
into fragments—

And yet, these Splinters of lost face,
lost life, lost heart, and lost hope
malinger in shallow, rocky
crevasses and open graves—waiting
ever so silently
as cleverly concealed yet piercing
impediments to all who certainly
will ask—moreover, will continue to ask—even
endlessly ask—

And in the sinister silence of the secular
Answer
other hearts and faces will surely
be torn.

That's

Yeah, "That's
right." I really do
understand—
because, yeah, at times
I can be "that's"—
as in "That's
harsh!" or "That's
rude!" or even "That's
it!"

So—I really can relate
to the unsettled sentiments that rage
uninspired and inarticulate
across the plasma ten-inch

set to mute—that's
your Face.

Many Hearts Were Beating

Many hearts were beating
in the Cardiac Surgery Recovery Room.

    duh-dum . . . duh-dum . . . duh-dum . . .

That was evident in the arrhythmic,
nervous conversation, that ended:
    "My son is in Guadalajara, in jail, and Grandma just
    sent $2,500 to bail him out."

    duh-dum . . . duh-dum . . . duh-dum . . .

The call "Grandma" had received was from India—
a scam, aimed at the sensitivities of the elderly;
it worked—

    duh-dum . . . duh-dum . . . duh-dum . . .

All that, as their fragile, little angel
with a tender, tiny, and broken heart
was deep in surgery.

    duh-dum . . . duh-dum . . . duh-dum . . .

Their son was safe, at home—yet
Grandma's money was in India, and the little
girl had her heart opened by the surgeon.

    duh-dum . . . duh-dum . . . duh-dum . . .

Grandma left before her granddaughter
ever awoke to chase the $2,500 in India—
from California—of course, to no avail.

duh-dum . . . duh-dum . . . duh-dum . . .

There is a *poignant* sadness hovering over *This World*
born of carelessness, thoughtlessness, and selfishness—
for there are men who prey on families with little girls

duh-dum . . . duh-dum . . . duh-dum . . .

who have broken hearts
that need mending.

I traffic in small fears . . .

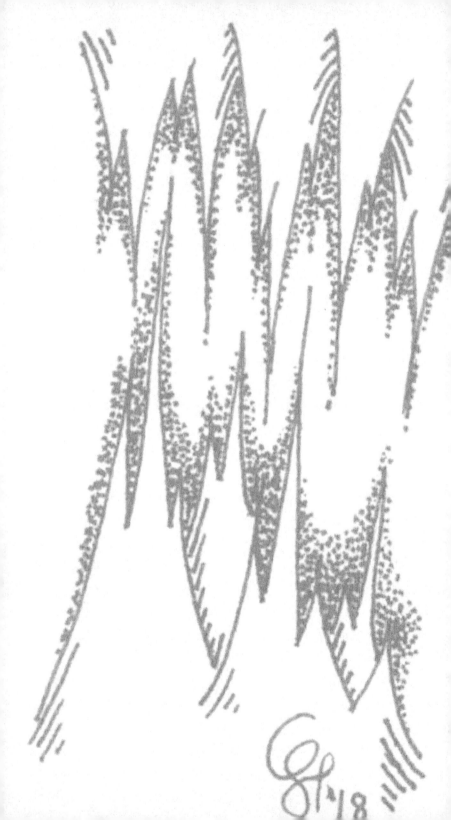

Small Fears

I traffic in *Small* Fears.

I am deaf with their Siren cries—

so demanding, shrill remanding—so *unwise*
    as to be noted, to be counted, to be incised
    inward, at the ledge's edge of my outward sill.

My flesh is wasted oft' in rivulets of halting tears
    for so many, many years, where they have worn
    my countenance stolid, stoic, and still—

my hopes—over-ground grist in its refining mill
    empowered by the harshest deluge, so forlorn,
    as to grind my dust to dust—for into dust,
    I am reborn

as my essential Fears:

    I fear rats in the attic and termites in the studs
    mold on the shiplap, imbedded bugs in the rugs

    cracks in the driveway and roots in the drains
    the tree that leans ever north in driving rains

    rot on my fruit trees, a ten-year fungus in the earth
    noises in my engine and a five-year moisture dearth

    funnel spiders in the lawn and wasps in the wall
    vacations and journeys whereupon my car might stall

        I fear stoic shrugs
            and periodic pains
        I fear insincere hugs

and tentative rains.

I fear difficult births
and intellectual fails
I fear piercing truths
and untraveled trails.

And so—

my past has made *this* very clear:
that unless my *angst* portends to fail,
I will yet find something to fear
in anything- and everything-at-all.

. . . and I remain there—
dreamless . . .

I Turn

I will usually commit
for a month or a year—
intending to live *real*, to care
large, to abandon fear
to change
true—

Then I turn from it
abruptly, suddenly—seemingly preferring
death
or at least elongated
sleep—

and *there,* I remain—
dreamless
apart

punctuated by an obtuse
incised and reckless
pain.

I Have Become

I once firmly believed that I was one
who was always *intended*
to be something other than the person
which I have since become.

Now, I just sit, stare, and wonder—
emotionally undone—
lost within the image that remains there
oblique yet emblazoned
within the one-way mirror
glass, which I have repeatedly shattered—
pleading for it to change . . .
    or fade . . .
        or fragment—
            far beyond my remembrance . . .

Yet—
it seems far too late
for me.

For no matter how deep
I search the sharp
edges of the shattered fragments
of mirror glass

I still see my likeness there—

and I am too grotesque
to be recognizable
even to the splinter.

Yes—

It appears

that even things
which have *gone to pieces*
have no need of me.

So, I cry—all the while
fingering through the fragments—
and I bleed.

Within the crimson smear, there comes
a change—The vulnerable in me wakes,
for as I continue to search within
those fragments, I stain
the glass shards with my life—it is strange
that they are so
gorgeous . . .

I look closer—
closer than I ever have before.
I suddenly see myself—
actually, a *truer*
version of myself within the telling
stain.

It is indeed—
magnificent.

It is unbelievably—
picturesque.

I, too, am broken and fragmented—
and in and about my Splintered
self, I am over and again
pierced and cut. I remain

fully blemished, still—

miraculously

I have become
beautiful.

The Answer

Tell me that
which I will never
need to hear.

Seal it
through a hardened whisper—
then, I will fear

   the answer

elaborated there, stamped within my eyes—

   the answer

still there—as incomprehensible, obvious lies.

Tell me—then
keep reminding me, daily—over and again
so that I will forget

what I see
what I know
what I feel
what I hear—

   the answer.

III.

Finding and Collecting the Pieces

The Buzzing Outside

I sat on my light cream, leather sofa and listened to it all—
to the children that *softly* sang the poisoned songs of both
the wasps and the yellow jackets as they tripped-buzzed by—
stingingly on striped skateboards and bikes and bright yellow
sneakered feet, and I then realized that all the pedestrian
traffic outside—the large and the small, the fast and the slow,
    the mean and the gentle, were venomous stingers
        driven intentionally,
        pulsatingly, deep into my soul's
        inert, dry earth.

Hope

Hope often flits about doorways
flickering in the dim glow of lamplights,
annoyingly offering me flashes of insight—
even fluttering clarification and explication
about Who I *Really* am.

So, I swat at it, and it withers—shivers
a single-winged dance, twisting and spiraling
down toward the earth—then while trembling
there, it periodically pulses with life—
vibrating tentatively upon the ground.

Often, I look upon it in its injured and fragile
state, considering what it must have intended
with its darting and buzzing *Grace*—there extended,
menacing and taunting me with future Bliss—
And I there and then stomp it lifeless.

It dies so often upon my floor—though it always
resurrects over and again, and no amount of Killing
can quell it eternally. Perhaps—someday, I might be willing
to *hear* it, to open myself fully to its fluttering Hope—
believing that *I* am a Soul, solitary, yet worth Saving.

Then Hope will never again be quelled—
And I will be both the harbinger and the harbor
of Hope, transfixed there upon that floor
destined and blessed to die no more—

Only to be Reborn
over and again—
eternally

as Peace.

Death Renounced

For a tad outside of twenty years now,
I have neglected living life, somehow—

I have inhabited that place, instead,
Which I call the vapid world of the dead—
for sadly, I have painfully often,
my simple youthful credo forgotten:

"I intermingle with the dead.
The dead can seem so alive,
but they're dead.

I know—

for I intermingle with the dead.
I've seen the dead try to imitate life—
but the stench of death can never be refuted.

Death is real.
I shall never be a part.

The dead may die a thousand times,
but I shall live forever."[13]

Thus—I now, intently renew my vow,
putting away my flaccid performance—
replacing acrid death with new birth now,
sealing it as focused grave avoidance—

If heaven—its hope—will here assist,
from recurrent death, I might be free—
from dearth of life and unconsciousness,

---

[13] "The Dead," a poem by Gregory D. Strawn, 1979

to die no more—to let *the morbid* be.

Though ensconced within weakness,
I will depart death's dismal din

and live a *true* life—

be *me*

once again.

. . . still water—
placid and calm.

Placid

I would gladly
trade myself
for something *grand:*
still water—
placid and calm.

Burning

As I have burned longer,
the flame of my incineration
has become vague and routine,

narrow in its focus—
warbling,
a passionless din—

a dreary, dim
dull light.

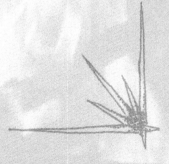

Perceptions Are Reality

Words are words—
meaningful, meaningless, indifferent.

Perceptions are reality—
biased, compassionate, passive, malignant.

And we choose carefully—
subconsciously, consciously, lightly, belligerently
    the parameters of our personal worlds,
    and we decisively inhabit these ecospheres

of our tact-ful-less creations—
veri-reality, veri-fantasy—in truth—both,

And then these faux perceptions
imperceptibly alter who we are in herstory and in history,
who others *have* been and *ever* will be—
how we might live
what we will love

And so we continue intently—
discontentedly or contentedly
    inhabiting our personal veri-fictional communities
    selected with selective, herstoric and historic intent.

And finally, filled with empty pride,
    when we are particularly careless inside,
we see through our Franken-life glasses,
    darkly—deceiving our own selves.

Manifestation of Elm

If I stand here too long,
my toes will begin to curl downward—
nails and cuticles and flesh
and tendons and bone,
piercing the moist topsoil—
which will soon inspire spontaneous
appendage bifurcation—
and I will become held-fast
at this spot, and no wind will ever, then,
move me,
and no rain will ever again
uproot me,

for I will be *Manifestation of Elm*

in the flesh—

All will see me
and Wonder.

. . . No rain will ever again
uproot me.

Post-Op Recovery

I am full empty
within the vacant expiration of this wheezy
exhale—a limp collapse
at the brittle edge of sense—
completely culpable, yet clearly incapable
of clarity.

So—I just sit and languish—
writhe and wince in poignant and peculiar
anguish.

After Dilaudid, I smile
and *love* deeper than I have ever loved
before—while

I fully understand
that I am still fuzzy
on the particulars
of being fuzzy on the particulars—
particularly as it relates
to my particular pain—

I merely occupy this place—
just sit here and take up space,
awaiting the latent sensation
of future regeneration—
of comfort and of clarity,
of full and complete sanity—

of pulsating, vibrant health.

Breath

I never would have believed
that the *simple* and underappreciated
act of breathing,
deep and constant—
would ever be a dire
difficulty
or even a painful
priority
for me.

In the past,
Inhalation and her
impulsive, compulsive sister,
Exhalation
always came to me—nagging me . . . so faithfully—
so very naturally—like, well—like
Breathing . . .

yet today, as I remember them both—
    their transparent beauty,
    along with their depth and breadth—
    their tickling, healing charity,
they have both forsaken and abandoned me
to the fearful tramping of the wheeze,
the choke, and the gasp—

Within this betrayal
I cautiously count all my breaths,
revering them as veiled
blessings
whenever they come
make a visit, even tentatively—
and I pray that they will remain

long
regularly
often

gifting my lungs power
    my brain clarity
    my limbs strength—

for lately,
the recalcitrant breath
in me does not always come
when she is called for,
and indolently
she chides and mocks, only periodically
affording me the release
from the gasp
I desperately need.

So very often she abandons me,
quits my lungs—and then
there is only faltering
    wheezing
    pausing
        intense spasms of grunts
    ceaseless coughing—

I ache,
straining to remember pure, unobstructed
    Breathing. Breath—
I tremble and sweat as I recall her visitations
    throughout my life,
during those seasons when I considered Respiration
as naught—for once upon a time,
I did not do *anything* to deserve her; she
just came to me.

She just came. She
was always there—
so faithful.

I will cherish every Breath
when I regain the gift of her presence
once more—and when I someday
take her again into my lungs—deep
droughts of sweet-smelling, oxygen-filled
Air—
so light and so long—and so regular and so
often,

I will be full—

for no mortal gift in all Creation is greater
than the regular and unhindered
gift of unimpaired
Breath.

She *is* Everything.

Seniors in the Fall

These raw, jagged Carving Blocks just sit there,

staring at me with their obtuse, blank, granite
    faces
tempered against whatever refining or chiseling I might
    attempt.
They dare me in their obstinate
    Vacancy
to "just try to shape" them
    with my Art.

Certainly, I understand the intended
innuendo in the overt challenge,
yet I cannot be dissuaded—

I continue to sculpt.

Realism, Romanticism, and Sincere
Artistry, in this, my chosen
Creative medium, are far too rare—
thus, many unfinished and rough
reliefs are released, yes, unfurled
    out into the vast, wide world.

Often, the slabs are dispassionately assaulted
instead of patiently and lovingly shaped—
They end up ground down or pulverized
instead of creatively chiseled and scraped,

resulting in being carried off and away on slight
winds as stone dust.

Then, as the particulates settle, they slowly build
layer by layer, mounding as rough lumps,

awkward and obtuse, transient bumps
on an otherwise inspired, pristine,
pleasant, and picturesque stone-
    scape—

And as a cause of even more distress,
on other occasions, the slabs are merely
shut-up and locked away—thoughtlessly
abandoned and warehoused as if useless—
flawed, unworkable rock,

saved for the outward insult of future *folk*
    renderings—*potential*

art—wasted—

wasted—

    Until when? Until when?

I ask . . . Then—
I ask, again . . .

    Until *when*?

There is no answer.

Still—even within this premeditated Silence
which captures and constrains my question—
And even though there is so much that contends
powerfully against me and against them,
I continue
    to sculpt—

And thus, as I proceed and persist
    within my daily carving, the chisel often slips

on the slick and rebellious stone.
    I, thereby, receive mortal wounds—

Indeed,
I am mortally wounded so often
that if looking forward, over the tops of the vast
contingencies of tentative monuments,
one might wonder if I am worn
    too thin
within the dying that comes so regular,
    like morning—
the death that I die over and over and over
    again.

It can never
stop, for I refuse to abandon
my calling—this art.
I am fixed in it.

I continue to sculpt.

Again and again, I swing the mallet
understanding that the many rebounding blows
that always unwittingly bleed me—like breath—
certainly will come. There will be no closure.

I will suffer this death
many times over
as I chip away at the many stoic slabs
and rough reliefs regularly placed before
me—imagining future glorious
    busts—
waiting on and praying for the occasional
    masterpiece.

I will continue to create—firm

in my belief that All artistic
renderings must eventually come
forth powerfully and magnificently—
Then even the art, itself, will realize *this*
about its own beauty:

    True art rises within the chips and blood and dust
        and death—
    Each finished relief is carved from the very life trust
        of the artist—

    And *that* life is always given away again and again
        freely, and with respect and hope and joyful remembrance
            of the carving, the chipping, the pain—

And so

in that day,
they, art and artists, will all bask together
within their individual and singular
beauties.

—strangely, they were
peace to me.

Random Egg-Throwing at Cars and Houses
A Conversation in My Mind

I continue to sit here, pensive, on my parent's porch, still accosted by the lingering, intermittent aroma of the raw eggs which I have just washed off my 81- and 85-year-old parents' car and driveway. It is Sunday morning—a day of rest—yet there has not been a moment of rest for my brother's wife, for me or my wife, for my siblings, for my parents, nor for our extended families. Instead, there have been many months of tears and aching and intense sadness.

Just minutes from here, in a baroquely decorated, shabby-sheik, surf-themed home with a wonderful ocean view of Torrance Beach, my elder brother is confined to a hospital bed, dying from a prolonged illness—brain cancer: glioblastoma. He has miraculously lived for almost seven years after having had part of his brain along with the original tumor removed, but it is a solemn reality that cancers nearly always find their way back—so it was for him. Now, he can barely talk, more-or-less move, and is terminally confined to that small hospital bed, having lost much of his once solid, strong, and sturdy muscle structure. We were all with him yesterday, remembering—sitting with him and remembering *so* much. It was nice being near him, sharing with him, thinking about how much we all love him—and remembering and reminiscing about his life and how his life had touched ours; it was also terrible, understanding that we all would soon be left on earth without his wit and without his casually majestic and powerful presence. He is still young, and I have so much more I want to experience with him.

*   *   *

While we slept (or attempted to sleep) last night, someone, perhaps selecting my elderly parents' home at random—yet acutely tragic in so choosing—this *someone* hurled a (most likely unintended) terrible and blatant insult at my parents during the most difficult time of their lives: losing their firstborn son to cancer. That fellow-Earth-sojourner may have just thought that it would be *fun* to throw eggs at some *old peoples'* house—my parents' home of fifty-two years. I cannot help but feel a bit of internal contention as I consider the tremendous scope and the deep, profoundly painful potential consequences of such a seemingly *small thing*—at "Random Egg-Throwing at Cars and Houses."

I check myself before my infant anger matures into rage, and I allow myself to ponder a bit upon the frail and flawed nature of *all* humanity, including those sad human tendencies toward self-serving, thoughtless insensitivity as well as self-righteous, provincial anger.

I have now calmed myself down—thinking does this—and my anger begins to subside, which is good. Anger isn't a useful emotion, anyway. It is a mere harbinger of ignorance and a manifest symbol of thoughtlessness. Today, I choose *reality* and *thought.*

*　　*　　*

After *all that is said and done*, I really do love my Savior—and later today, in His name, I will beg, again, for forgiveness of my own sins and weaknesses, which I have once more, thoughtlessly, strewn across the lawn of my week. There are also shells and yokes there, along with the putrid aromas of both occasional as well as habitual failures across the landscape of *my* life—self-vandalism. My Savior forbears anger against me, and instead, He will again grant me reprieve for another week—as He has every week of my past—showing me both grace and love, as I honestly recommit to *try* to square my life with His will—over and again. I have never been fully successful in my efforts to be the man I promised I would become, but I do continue to try. Today, I will gratefully partake of the Sacrament of my Lord's Supper, and He will forgive me and grant me another chance. How kind. How patient.

Patience. Kindness.

This analogy came to me earlier, as I was hosing down my parents' car and scrubbing the egg off of it with a stiff brush before re-hosing it, over and over—for egg, like weakness, thoughtlessness, and sin, sometimes requires multiple scrubbings—often over time—and with inestimable elbow-grease, along with significant patience, before the ability to finally overcome becomes real, as well as for the consequences of some redundant recalcitrances to finally come all-of-the-way off. Even now, I understand more clearly, as the unpleasant aroma of the wet egg lingers about me, that sometimes, the stench of our own weaknesses and misdeeds also lingers on and on and continues to stink-up our lives—because we are, after all, mostly weak, myopic, and imperfect—mortals.

As I continue to consider the unprecedented patient and kind nature of Christ's Atonement, along with my own persistent and hardened weaknesses, I no longer feel any anger at all toward the thoughtless (most likely) youth who had made such a (seemingly) razor-edged, and certainly uncalculated, error in judgement—just sad. I am sad at the ignorance and carelessness that hurls, without thought, such insensitive, heart-piercing Splinters and insults, yes, at my parents, but also, all around the wide world. It is even more disheartening to me as I realize that, at some level, this thoughtlessness exists within all of us—so many weak, and at times, selfish, human beings, randomly, unknowingly, and metaphorically, kicking the downtrodden and tripping the feeble and spitting upon the weak—and even throwing eggs at the elderly couple who live up the hill—at the very moment their firstborn son is dying. Yes, this frailty really does exist within each of us—so within the haze of our own foibles, we cannot reasonably or fairly judge others with any real accuracy, even when the offense seems so *cut-and-dried*.

I suddenly recall the many times when I, myself, had been a recipient of the same treatment which was tossed at my parents last night. I also remember a conversation I had, many years ago, after mentioning to my brother how sad it made me when my students would vandalize *my* home with eggs. That conversation was with my elder brother, the same brother whom I love so deeply, who right now is dying in his home.

He responded: "That's not really a big deal. We all did that to our teachers when we were in high school."

It caught me off guard; I never had done that. Still, according to that logic, because I am a teacher, perhaps it should have been understandable to me, or perhaps, I even *deserved* it for my choice of occupation. My parents, though, are not teachers; it is, therefore, not understandable to me, and they definitely do *not* deserve it. They are an elderly couple who spends countless hours baking bread and cookies and preparing meals for others and making visits to the homes of those who are old and sad and lonely within their community. They are concerned about and take care of those around them, even when they, themselves, are also in need of help.

At a more immediate and provincial level, I am even more deeply saddened as I wonder at the ignorance of so many in society who take this natural thoughtlessness, of which we are all capable, to unnatural and more vicious levels—the violence that exists within the hearts and minds of these individuals who not only inflict this kind of pain, but who *enjoy* doing so; they are the ones who often will return in order to watch the people who they have hurt—to observe them suffer within the trauma that they have inflicted upon them. And then, when there is another opportunity, they often will do it again— and even *again*.

*   *   *

One week later: This is, perhaps, what has happened to my parents, for today is another Sunday, just one week after the first egging, and I am repeating the same exercise—this time, it is likely only hours, or at most days, until my brother will die—and I am washing the second round of smelly disrespect from my parent's car. This renewed uncivil wrong is clearly an act of ignorance, even more than one of unkindness. This ignorance, perhaps, comes from a general societal numbness of heart, paralysis of conscience, and a lack of love and caring—perhaps the result of poor, or even non-existent, teaching by parents, or even teachers—who else could be held responsible for neglecting to educate young ones about what is right and what is wrong, as well as compassion and kindness, if not parents and teachers? Still, so many adults, it seems, do not fulfill this fundamental, fiduciary responsibility, and, therefore, so many children just "do what[ever they] want." Someday, I believe, every one of us will come to realize that discipline is tantamount to love— that it is the same thing. There is no love without discipline. There is no growth without love.

Regardless of where the failure to teach *right and wrong* or *compassion and kindness* to children, exists, it is a monumental failure with terrifying and perhaps eternal consequences.

I will not tell my parents about the back-to-back Sunday eggings, for it would merely add insult to their injury—and the present injury is just too great to have it expanded upon. It must simply be left alone. I shudder when I think: *What if I were not here to wash the eggs off their car and down the gutter? What, then, would the net result of that careless act of egging have been? What if my parents— who are in mourning, who are weak and feeble themselves—what if they had gone out to their car, today or last Sunday, to head on over to be with their dying son?* They would have, sadly, had an untenable choice: either to postpone that trip in order to clean up the mess that was so ignorantly and thoughtlessly thrust upon them—missing precious time with their son—or they might have just left it alone and allowed their car's paint to become destroyed—then they would have had with them for as long as they owned that car, damaged paint as a remembrance of that insult, which was thrown at them, right as their son was dying—a permanent and perverse monument to their life's greatest pain.

*   *   *

I remember another occasion, well over fifteen years ago. I had returned home from a long trip with my family. It was late—past midnight. My middle daughter, who was eleven, had been having problems with her bones and teeth for months. She would break her bones with very little impact, and her teeth were loose and beginning to fall out, and we didn't understand what was happening to her, so we had been waiting to find out the results of some medical tests that would provide answers. As we pulled up in our van with five sleepy children inside, we noticed that someone had egged *our* house during our absence. There were dozens of eggs, strewn all over our newly painted house and siding and driveway. I started cleaning it up and hosing things off and scrubbing the hardened eggs. It became clear that the eggs had been there for days, and that the damage would be permanent. As I was working to clean it up, my wife listened to a message on the answering machine and then came outside to tell me that my daughter's test results were back, and that she had been diagnosed with a bone disease that caused her bones and teeth to weaken and disintegrate. We were devastated by the news, and within that devastation, I continued to clean up the insult of the eggs—for hours, into the early morning, crying for my sick daughter—while taking note of the permanent reminder, the paint-scarring, from the eggs.

The next day, after having taught a full day at high school, I went to teach my evening college classes. While teaching at the college that night, I collapsed into a chair, and I could not move. I could not speak clearly, only mumble. I could not lift my arms. I had become paralyzed. My students left me there, and I sat alone for quite a while—until I was finally able to get the attention of a familiar student who had walked by my empty classroom—for the second time. Realizing that something was not right with me, she asked if I needed help; I made eye contact, and she came to my aid. She called my wife. Later, it was determined that I had experienced a fairly serious anxiety attack—brought on by the tremendous stresses and trials of life—all punctuated, with an *exclamation mark*, by the eggs.

In truth, we all do damage to others fairly regularly, without always knowing it, without even trying. We, therefore, should be patient and kind, no matter the context or the severity of the offence, offering grace to each other, for we will often need that same grace, from others whom we have offended, ourselves. We are Splinters in others as others are Splinters in us. It does no good to keep score, just to remain kind.

Still, it would be wise to avoid adding to the pain that we *unintentionally* cause others by carefully avoiding committing premeditated, metaphorical "Random Egg-Throwing at Cars and Houses."

The Buzzing Inside

I sat there, safe, curled up within my thoughtful, yet quiet, mind—
listening cautiously to the black buzzing of the bumble and the hornet
and even the common horse fly—and it was all so horribly
simple—so naturally mundane, that I remained fixed in my place—
questioning neither the bite nor the sting, even though they pierced
the intent of my neutrality and caused me to question
    my purpose,
        my reality, my past, my future . . .

    . . . I there and then
felt both the sting and the bite
        anew—

Strangely, they were
peace to me.

And I love you
more essential than I realized
was possible . . .

IV.

The Mosaic

I Finally Saw *You*—

When I walked by you this evening
for the hundred-thousandth time,
    after thirty-eight years of daily
    walking past you—

I saw *you*.

You were really no different from how
    I had seen you before,
    except for the wear-and-tear
    of thirty-seven years of you
    walking by me—

Yet, somehow, incarnate—
I finally *saw* you.

It was my heart which saw you first—

    a spontaneous arrhythmia erupted,
    shooting pointed darts of intense, oxygenated energy
    deep, pulsating through my heart, firing up
    at least twelve—of my eight—
    cylinders, obviously overwhelming
    my newly enlightened equilibrium.

It then electro-shocked my brain into a transformation—

    wherein, my mind became the sharpened
    statistical enumeration of each
    rapid heartbeat and elated emotion,
    even as it surged inward, overcoming the empirical
    by transforming into the diamond-dimension
    of my very soul,

which soul perceived you next—

And that soul?

It grew into a soft ache
engorged with memory and emotion,
which poignant and pleasant pain swelled
all throughout the evening

becoming an essential and scintillating
suffering—

which suffering continues
still.

Deceit II

While we sat there at the seashore,
    silently—upon
damp sand,

I envisioned new hope,
    for I trusted in your nature.

Then—

There was a sudden rumbling within the sea
    calling after both you and me—
And the retracting tides took us both.

Yet—

even though I was forever swept away
from that beach upon that day—

    somehow

I still found a way to both pen and publish

    this poem.

The Wind-Sculpted Pines

I was weary from shore-wandering—
captured in the torrential side winds
that raged until near collapse:

The Pines, the Bodies, their tenured pasts—
all fell—slowly, methodically reclining
impossibly tilting to the East—

Held there in essential Tableaux
as the sober Spirits of Men blew past—
heads held down to divert their Bending.

I remained Curled tight, my eyes closed—
Thus, seeing more clearly Those intangibles
who in their fluttering merely passed on—

Twisting at tortured right angles, the distorted
horizons, Bodies, and trees were more natural
than Straight sight could discern—

And I could sense the evolution of reality
in the Blind Contortionism of those Shoreline Pines,
waiting eternally for the flutter to Move them.

Baptism

The ocean calls to the true believer—
As he answers—bows beneath the waves
in reverence and sacred cleansing,
filled with awe—he is reborn.

The Chalice

Yes, my son—my dear
boy, I am still here
drinking from this tarnished chalice.
Yet, it is now so very clear—
that I must also share
it with you.

How can I both drink and give drink
simultaneously
without spilling the precious elixir of life
between us?

    (I know from experience—
    I don't look good with life
    dribbling from my chin.)

Still, as it is my joy and duty so to do,
I will pass the cup on to you—

Where we will hold it together for a time,
understanding that as we sip—
both of us yet unrefined,
some of the liquid will likely slip
onto our clothes and then to the ground—
wasted.

Still, we must drink here
    now,
together—

for when this cup is baren inside
so, also, is our time—
your time and my time—to share.

Know this, my son, that my chokings and splatterings
are all unintentional,
and that which I drink and dribble
is for the natural
love, which I feel for you.

I do apologize—
for it is very true
that, at times, you
will be spilled upon
because when life's
cup is shared, messes
as well as successes
will come to light.

My son,
I will soon finish my drink—
You will still have many hence.

I pray that this chalice which we share
will always, for you, be filled with care
and also with the sweetest of draughts—
that your drink will be pleasant and long,

and that your splatterings, dribblings, and spillings,
    will be softer than mine—
yet also shared with your son.

Perhaps the three of us, someday, will
    drink, dribble, splatter, and spill

together.

Lights

The dim, amber lights
hung low on that final
horizon within the fragile fragment of time—
pale and unnatural within the opaque fog
which held them there.

In that essential haze,
their shards of sharp
illumination were more dull than bright,
and they suffered within that dimensional
confusion as do all

terrestrial things—
stalwart beings—

who desire the deeper
burning of Celestial insight
even as they strain in agony
against the dimming of the light
within the telestial sphere
of their consignment.

My Son

You are a wonder from God
which I have always hoped I might be—
In that, the gift that you are, my son—
I can believe that, perhaps, there is peace for me.

Oh! That a man like me
should have such a son—
the son you have chosen to be.

Sandra D.

Should it have been expected of
    me
to walk upon this Earth all
    alone—
more than once, I would have
    stumbled
headlong into the cavernous
    sinkholes
that pepper the shorelines of my
    life
and, tragically, I would have been
    lost.

Rattlesnake Grass at Westport Union Landing

The fragile stalks of rattlesnake grass
shake and bounce with the hollow burden of their tightly wound
    coils
striking and retracting in the pulsating wind
fragilely, failingly, and falteringly at gnats and moths and lady bird
    beetles—

Recently commissioned by Spring
to rise from the moist earth as serpentine sentinels
before drying to straw
then rescinding as vagabonds,
escaping over the ragged ridges of the crumbling
cliff faces—

a playground for white, yellow, and orange
    butterflies
    that wobble and twist about the coils
    imposing mating dances—
a flight line for black hawks and brown eagles
    that lightly brush their breast feathers
    against the rattle-less rattles
    as they hunt the cliffs for reptiles and rodents—
as well as a terrestrial
    low-way for transient sea gulls and purposeful pelicans
    as they ride the up-wind to and from their chosen
    feeding grounds—
an intellectual and most effectual internal de-noculation
    for emerging poets and reluctant artists who thrive here, even
    among the tossings within their thick skulls and about
    their passionate and eurythmic hearts.

These inspiring occupiers of ocean cliffs are indeed
    odd—
inverted creature facsimiles,

stealthy fangs buried deep below the surface—
    rooted
as firmly as anything could ever take root in the rocky,
chalky layer of sediment
and stone—
    and from there,
they slither with purposeful intent absolutely
nowhere,
living only delicately
in the here-and-now,
bouncing and shaking their benign rattles

enthusiastically,
though earth-fettered,

in the surging and halting force
of the erratic
    wind.

for the seashore . . .
inspires manifest philosophical
Clarity . . .

Ocean Culture

The pulverizing power
infused with the impressive
obsessive
incessant pull
    of the crushing and surging ocean surf,
        in truth
is reflective and refined—
wonderous, vibrant,
absolutely unrestrained—
as it tugs at individual grains
    of sand
sifting them, choosing them

as it also sifts, chooses, and refines
those restless wayfarers
    called *home* to its saline shores—

those relentless recreants

who forever claim the ocean's
    swells and shallows,
tidal estuaries and wind-sculpted sand
    canyons,
surf-carved cliffs and wafted
    waves,
mollusk eaten rocks and low tides' rewashed
    treasures
        as their home—

Theirs is an eclectic culture
of sensation and thrill, kelp and brine,

of scattered shells and cold unrest, fine

sand and calculated unease,
chilling wind and simplistic peace—
of spume and spray, engendering serenity,
severity and causal creativity—
of small stones, of sand crabs and labored breath,
youth and credulity

    and microscopic death—

which tentatively lingers
visceral in the fragile, dissipating fingers
of foam, winding egg yolk
yellow and irregular, day after day after day
along this coast, which repetitively evokes
reflection at the moist rim of its bay—
meditation on the sand, drifting ever
slowly, on into forever—

of mildew, sunburned backs and faces,
shipwrecks and truncated strife,
laminated thoughts' traces

    and macroscopic life—

brimming right there
in the calculated and concentrated,
simple yet *knowing* over-stare
retaining the surfers:
    mentally reaching outward
    spiritually intuiting inward
    physically moving forward
        always focused the inverse of shoreward—
to the waves, and even
past the waves—

sea-feeling further seaward, after those *other* waves

which in their infancy are slight
    ripples—
Then intuiting even further
outward, to the essences of waves
which are beyond the *formed* waves and behind those *other*
    waves—
still, always searching to those *embryonic* waves,
    still undeveloped,
    unformed—
yet fully comprehended, spiritually realized, if not actually
divined, by these magnificent shore-sojourners—
the oceans' husbandmen—tamers and masters,
cutters and shapers
of the natural falling and plummeting
of the swells and surges.

And all of that intuitive extending
and emotional blending of man with the swells that brake
and the recycling tidal surf that takes
individual grains from the shore's cache of filtered sand
and returns them to the sea—

Well—

it changes the boy or the man or the memory of the man
who in his shore-wonderings,
in essence

is really, mostly, a boy—

for the seashore
along with its harvest of waves
    and wayfarers and sand-sifters
inspires manifest philosophical
    Clarity,
produces passive oceanic communal

Sympathy,
fulfills artistic passion, within
awe-filled respect and honor—even

Mana

which trammels as it travails deep
as sober, selected truth
within and throughout all sculpted

Waves

and around and about all tested and selected

Wave-riders.

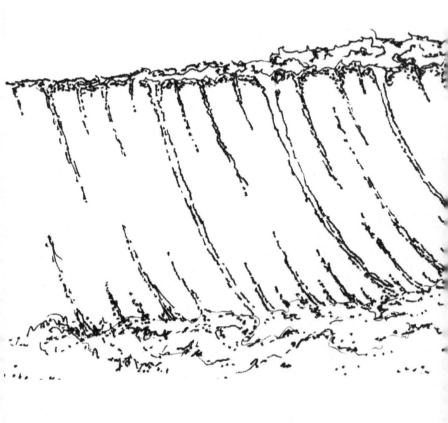

. . . awaiting another upsurge
of the powerful ebb and flow—

Wind at Westport

We forgot to pack a kite
again this summer, I now realize,
and the wind here is so strong—
just *perfect* for sailing the skies
and we haven't sky-fared in so long—
so we think a bit, then we improvise
before the picturesque day is gone
and settle for a suitable substitute—

watching the butterflies erratically flit
as they make their purposeful passes,
tap lightly at the heads of the impatient
mostly dry, tense, and restless grasses
which lurch and bend erratically as they ride
back and forth before they swerve
carelessly from this to that side
in the rampant, recurrent surges—

where we observe the black hawk sentinels
catch the stern drift-force winds, surfing
the ocean-eroded cliff ledges below,
whereupon they pause in their soaring
enjoying the power of the ebb and flow—
while in another upsurge, a few imposing
pelicans drop in from the outside, riding
the ridges and swells of the tidal winds—

lifting, undulating, falling, and flapping
until they finally disappear before our eyes
around that last rugged rock outcropping
where they certainly own the sunburst skies—
Still, they also take the ocean, descending low
dragging their bills through the crests
of the rough surf, as they patiently troll

somewhere along the Lost Californian Coast.

Even though, in their might,

these tidal winds are belligerent
    tent-brakers
and tablets-of-poetry-and-sketches-
    takers,

we are all awed by them.

I am quite certain that we will
    forget
to pack our kites once again
    next year.

. . . desperate to stamp
individual marks
indelible on water, on air,
on sand.

The Bacon Within

I whittled a solitary slice of smoked bacon
out of a slight sliver of the rotting walnut
stump (which I had painstakingly
dug up and pulled out of our backyard
before leaving it there to cure for a decade),
the one that Mike chopped into firewood
for our evening campfire in the redwoods—

and when I peered deep into the grain
of that fragment of rich velvety brown,
which did not burn, but merely settled
into the dark compost beneath the trees,
I saw only bacon—and I, of course, was drawn
to turn that vision into concrete reality
with my whittling and shaping and sanding,

and slowly, carefully, I urged
into existence this singular curly, wavy, crispy
slice of fried bacon—animal from vegetable,
food from fuel, breakfast from evening
snack—and art from discarded, misunderstood
refuse, and I now always keep it near me—
just in case I feel incessant pangs of hunger.

Waves At Westport

Persistent, belligerent
they press—one by one—
by one,
elucidating their monotonous and angry
roars, ever desperate to stamp
their individual marks
indelible on water, on air,
    on sand—
on man.

Open-mouthed and drooling, they brake.
Frothing, they howl shoreward, lips curling,
spitting a fine mist,
growling both south and north—
roiling, fraught with intensity and power,
rolling and tumbling and swirling
before their frothy
wakes close together in inert,
foamy spumes,
    consuming each other
    completely.

Therein exhausted, they regurgitate over
and over, mixing their individualities
    with sand and kelp
and, of course, the memory
of that eternal
moment—
playful repetition, replete
with endings only moments apart
from beginnings—

denouement.

. . . and all the deterioration from time
become the salt of joy,

for I love you.

I Love You More

The affection that I feel today
deepens, folds, then stretches like thin
wrinkles of age
embossed on the limitless planes
of eternity,
and I find perennial rest there—
in time
in immortality

In You—

And I love you
more essential than I realized
was probable
more intense than I understood
was possible—
and all the pains of aging
and all the deterioration from time
become the salt of joy,

for I love you.

. . . becoming knowing
and force, gravity and orbit,
light and its warmth

V.

The Cure for All Wounds

Love Casts Away Fear

When I was a child, I frequently
hid from the omnipresent
manifest many—
    the onerous schoolyard bullies.

They first challenged my physical
power—which was at best, less
than weakness—and at worst, feral
    foolishness.

They next confronted my emotional
security—which was, in a word, *in*security—
and if within a telling and insightful
poem—full and relentless cacophony.

So I shielded my fragile
soul, and became lost—swept
inside my own swollen,
crimson eyes—for I wept.

My heart accelerated, then leapt—
    revved in neutral before it
    stalled—and thereafter fell apart.

I tried to remain invisible, or at least
    opaque,
but I was always so completely
    obvious—

and so, day after day
    week after week
    year after year—
No matter how *in tableau* or how still I stood,
No matter how distant from society I drifted,

I was always discovered and caught
    then democratically Stung—
        Me, it seemed, alone against Everyone.

Over and again, I was overcome—
Pierced and then re-pierced by the splintered
shrapnel of that singular

Fear:

    not conforming within a world
        of similars,
    owing that fact to my being found
        dissimilar

        peculiar.

That knowledge, *understood*, informed
my childhood, wherein I reticently
disbanded my futile hopes for sociality.
Confusion owned my peace and fettered
my faith—I was continually hopeless.

Within *my* memory, I was imprisoned,

for my reality remained relentless.

Fear shattered my focus, my drive,
as well as any *perceived* power inside—
which I may have ever wished
to be real, and I sincerely believed
that I could do nothing to restore
my refracted hope, once more.

I was not, in truth,
as were the *others*: social, confident, strong, interesting, stable,

normal—

Still, that irregular and fettered state of mind
which was clearly, undeniably mine
was never *natural*
to me—yes, it was *odd*—
for, I was, after all
royalty—a true son of God.

There should have never been fear,
no terror, within me—

ever—

yet and alas,
thus and alack,

> there it was
> there it existed—
> there it reigned
> there it persisted—

deep inside of me—for years
festering through my heart,
moldering within my gut,
shrieking about my ears.

Inside of myself—it was ever strung-out,
unaccountable and harsh, there were so many tears—
growing, enlarging, constraining, expanding

for so many, many years . . .

> And there was also fettered fear in Salem, four
> full centuries before my boyhood trauma—

189

a hardened, malignant, and unaccountable fear
that writhed within mortals and rose above
    all other fears—
Birthed across the many waters[14]
as a heretic-laced religiosity—powerfully
dramatic in rash response to pseudo-faithful
    faithlessness,

sharpened and turned inward—an uncertain tension
impaling the very heart of truth and mind of reason—
compressing and constraining a pure and ancient
    innocence,
forcing it to cower there as surreal, exploited, archaic
    foibles,
misperceived, compounded, then exaggerated as social
    evils.

I have also been run through by misperceptions
    even casual, self-sustaining exaggerations—
wounding *me* to avoid consequence, a part
    of my past—before my *true* life's start—
therefore, unfettered to all actionable
    realities—forever remaining miles apart
from all practical, material truth or spiritual
    understanding or psychological

    consideration—for actuality
    can never exist fully

within any faux or fantastical
bifurcation of truths—
including those *truths* that flail
as incessant mania, even
as they constrain

---

14 An allusion to Revelation 17:15

creativity
and inundate mundane
individuality

for in fallaciousness' attempt to manipulate,
it provokes Suffocation—along with her odious
offspring: all of the many passively
invoked Fears.

And thus, shards of strained veri-fiction callously
call forth entrenched
Weakness
effectually exude
Sadness,
spreading Infectious
Tears—

as they always have,
as they always do,
as they always will—

Tears which always weep
even more tears, still—
a weeping which trammels up
by necessity, tangential
and askew from reality,
even more and more
caustic Fears,

and such Fears rise and then conjure
as they deign to expand,
intending to thrive within and throughout for
many generations,
as sinister designs for the destruction of human

Peace.

So—murder and deceit, pride and mayhem—
    Along with other sordid Stains,
marred Salem—not unlike they did in Jerusalem,
    its namesake, wherein the pains
which marred First Innocence was First
    sacrificed.

Still—

there would ever be additional
insurrections, assaults against innocence
in the ensuing two thousand years since—
leading into the breeding of the twenty-
twenty plague—of manic misinformation—

and within fewer than two myopic years . . .

    That illness? The tears? The misplaced
        violence and irrational fears,
    they assaulted and embraced me—
    Without my consent
        they consumed what yet remained in me,
    ignoring my dissent.

    And therein arose a narcissistic
        justice,
    a reactive, hostile, audibly sick
        anger
    brandished on the cuff of perceived
        partisan plots:
            intolerant outcries against so many injured
                souls
            including against my own splintered
                soul.

It was manifest in the flesh: friends, co-workers, strangers—

For these myopic many crushed their fellow-sufferers,
the oblique *others*, including *fragmented me,*
into *air*, even vacuous near oblivion—
before ever so carelessly,
    with backhanded simplicity,
        stitching us back up, though loosely—
            leaving the seeping and the weeping
                wounds open to the acrid air—oozing—
                    so that the traumas would never fully heal,
                but upon us, about us, and within us, prevail
            pushing rhetoric away, pushing me away,
        forcing me to leave myself—all alone
    without any hope, miles each day—
from the *real* me, from *This One*,
    and in the end, they

even replaced me—

and within the confusion of their insidious, interior motif,
fallacy continued to thrive, for it had malignantly survived

and after their audacity had replaced me, it then dismissed

    Who I was
    What I was
    How I was—

and thereby made it easy, eventually, although painful to me,
    to erase me—

It erased even

    me.

Yet through my ethereal spirit,
I still could perceive
an insidious deceit, which led to an overthrow

    of kindness
    of tolerance
    of peace—

as all the while, they cleverly invoked the sacred names

    of kindness
    of tolerance
    of peace—

thereby Resurrecting Salem's fear, the fear found
throughout ancient Jerusalem, along with my personal
childhood fear upon that primary school playground—
therein Restoring hatred—an inexplicable, unaccountable
intolerance against social introversion,
revealed intuition
perceived as weakness—

Bias disguised as equity and justice—
    kindly calling good evil and evil
        good, reigniting

ancient emotions, resurrecting
encumbering childhood fears
by discounting—

    What *I knew*
    What *I felt*
    Who *I was*—

With restrained triumph, they ripped out my tears,

dug through my heart, tore up my mind—
          enlarging their voices by dismissing mine,
               feeding my frustration with further

          Fears—

and while hidden
underneath my fallen countenance
even within all that confusion
and piercing pain—
hope still came

     to me—

     It returned even to me.

Also love returned
as severe as innocence

     as it always does
     as it always will
     as it always has

to Jerusalem, to Salem, to the playground
     at Calle Mayor School,
even to the vilified victims of the *Brave New* Covid
     World[15]—

And as I linger and am lost
within those stray and redundant
     thoughts,
And as I tremble through the understanding
which leads to clarity
in the reminding:

---

[15] An allusion to the novel *Brave New World* by Aldous Huxley

I was not the first
        to bleed
I would not be the last
        to bleed
and that I will most certainly
        bleed again,

I simply smile—

I also therein recall
through some ethereal gift of private
        conscience
that my God had held me before—
        even
comforted me
        on that Playground of Pretense
        in the Crucible of the Classroom
        along all my fear-riddled roads

        to Peace.

As unappreciated, as misunderstood as I may be—
And as fearful as that may be for me—

    Know this,
    Believe this, my soul,
    believe This—

Love casts away fear.

In Heaven, There is No Fading

Regular fading will always persist
here in mortality—consistently.

You have seen it, and so have I.

Redundant and with such regularity—
    all life, through which we persevere,
    pulse and breath, we so revere—
        eventually,
        both dry and die.

For even the purest of mortal Souls, mirrors
the path of the sun-drenched, yellow flower.
Although vibrant and bright in youth,
once cut away from the soil, her
    essential, connective truth—
if she is persistently there left,
    of water forever bereft—
she cools, browns, and fades,
    degrades within days.

Yes, both souls and flowers
    must drink from living water
        to retain their full colors
            bright, upon the earth.

Still—there forever remains
    this telling and compassionate truth:

In heaven, there is no fading.
Eternity is covered completely
in living water, forever endowing
the withered with new life—Free,
Crisp and Beautiful.

Undertow

As I shore-wander, slowly
    wincing,
all the while, thoughtfully
    pulling
at the proud tide's damp
    tracks—
which first rise up and then seep
    back—
retracing steps through the paths of my mind,
while searching longingly, lovingly, and deep—
even passionately within the intimate and refined
sticky-tacky, fine-lace tapestry
    of ocean wave overspray,
I begin to understand the roiling and the raging
    that has always existed in this place,
right there, just offshore, underneath that undulating
    surface—

And I've come to realize that this marvelous ocean
has always worked its fierce, slow malevolence
achingly upon us all. I am reminded of the stinging brine
that swells and surges through each life, and I grimace
as I recollect the sea's dark places:

    the acrid red tides which shuttle
        death
    the riptides that drag souls far out
        to the depths.

I marinate in them All

as I remember Kirt—
my big brother, who answered
    this ocean's, this shore's, manifest call—

his life, his will, his heart—for art.

Within my life, he purposely infused
this sea, and it also became *my* refuge.

Kirt's meaningful play was right here, surf-riding
the great-great-great grandparents of these very
waves, even as he basked in the refreshing
ocean mist overspray
across his face while he sat upon the arcing
    swells,
deeply awed, reflecting upon their many
      marvels.

He selected each wave
to personally tame
riding all the chosen,
    ancient breaks—day
        after day, week after
            week, month after month,
                year after year—lifetime
after lifetime.

And all the while, it remained right there—right with him—
that triangular reach of the riptide, the red tide, and the eternal
tug of the undertow—the same underpull which continually swam,
while he sat upon the sea's surface—unnoticed, beneath him—

pulling at him,
    pulling at me,
        pulling at us all—eternally
pulling us slow, though with design,
    past the spray, through the rip,
        over the red, within the brine
            out to the wonderous depths,
                far out into the supernal sea.

The Word

I must plunge through the nearest portal—wormhole
to the earth's emblazoned, primeval germination
on the most fortuitous wave of the galaxy's
undulating ribbon of time and space

And therein *hear* the vast something-ness
of the not-much-yet-ness of the matter-essence
that has become all that I now feel.

I need to *know* the proto-micro-miniscule particles'
dance to compression—a drastic, warping twist
toward implosion—becoming knowing and force,
gravity and orbit, light and its warmth.

I feel to *see* the pulsating centripetal swirl
that transfigured potential, particular matter
into neutronic, electronic, protonic, and magnetic material—
pre-primordial atomic structures,
compressed and melded into molecular patterns—elementally—

And then experience the multitudinous reactions—
as simple chemicals, metals and acids, bases and gasses
interact, ignite, are drawn together, then ripped
apart—repetitively exploding and imploding,
surging and resisting—gaining in complexity
to become the womb of all life, the futurity
of all death—the proto-nuclear molecular ancestors of all
that is, that sustains, that relieves . . . being—

And I will feel these as they combine and divide,
whip and whirl, then blast and blaze; thus
The Word: uncreated—Still Creating—Is Spoken,
and I will see and hear and know embryonic Earth—

and peer deeply into its reversing, magnetic, polar
past—before Pangaea[16]—and even before the seething
ridges of the oceans' depths obediently began dispatching
their lurching molten cores shoreward, and before
that dense conveyance with its ancient, weighty load
was thrust down, even deeper beneath the Son-Lighted
surface—

Intently re-refined—travailing and traversing currents,
bequeathing holocausts unimaginable to the stubborn
shales, conglomerates, and heavy ores, melting
as mammon to magma, until thereafter—Redeemed,

Heaving up a new terrain—powerfully Justified,
forged—folded, pounded, stretched, and Cleansed
as peerless Steel—immovable Monuments to
Creation, Timelessness, Value, Refinement,

Redemption; thereafter, eternally testifying boldly
indeed—

In The Word.

---

[16] A theoretical landmass that is said to have existed 300 to 200 million years ago, from
which all the present continents of Earth came

—powerfully Justified,
forged—folded, pounded, stretched, and Cleansed . . .

Afterword

Interestingly enough, I have discovered through the lengthy living of my life that the shattering and the splintering along with the pain that inevitably comes therein and therefrom are positives in my life—yes, I did say positives. I am eternally grateful that I have had sadness and suffering, as well as doubts, fears, and failures. I am thankful for traumas and frustrations and missteps and muddlings. They have all led me to discover the joy that eventually rises within, throughout, and beyond the trials, along with the deeper understanding, the knowledge and clarity—the restorational residue of working through hard things, patiently over the process of time. Difficulties have also helped me develop a firm faith in the goodness of God and have opened my eyes to recognize the beauty within the occasional triumph of simple success. I am thankful for having had the opportunity of being misunderstood, misrepresented, mistreated, and forsaken as well as having been respected, appreciated, and supported. These experiences have been the nutrients of my life, and they have nourished me, teaching me understanding, kindness, hope, faith, fidelity, and—patience—well, at least I am beginning to understand patience. Someday, as my struggles continue to intensify, I believe I will be able to grasp it tight and hold on to it, too, and eventually even incorporate it fully into my life.

So—I am thankful that I have lived an imperfect life, for because of my imperfections, I have searched for respite and redemption, and in that search, I have found a warming peace, for I have discovered slight slivers of goodness within myself; I have found beauty, understanding, and opportunity in both the small differences and cavernous divides between me and others; and in and about the telling, reflected images and recurring trauma found within the ever persistent Splinters, I have found God.

Photographs and Artwork

I created all artwork, took all photographs, and designed and organized all of the elements between the front and the back covers of this collection of poetry. I also took the photographs for the covers, but my daughter, Kayla Eshbaugh, designed them.

Acknowledgments

I love my patient and supportive wife, Sandy. She is my life partner, my eternal love, my confident, my counselor, my mentor, my sounding board, my stabilizer, and my best friend. It has been a privilege to spend the past 38 years with her and to fail and to succeed and to learn and to age together. We should have many more years together in this life, and we intend to remain together in eternity as well. She is my "Dream Girl." I love you, Sandra D.

I am blessed to have ten talented children (I always include both my biological children as well as my children-in-law when I speak of "my children") who are so capable in their chosen vocations and advocations, who have placed their families at the center of their lives and are such wonderful examples and parents to my many grandchildren. They are all good people—making the world a better place just by *being*. They are my friends, and we care about and help each other. They support me in my art. I am so blessed to have them in my life, and I love them all.

My middle daughter, Kayla Eshbaugh, who is a photographer, an artist, a designer, and a published author of novels, novellas, children's books, and a writing guidebook, is the artistic designer for the covers of my books of poetry, as well as my production and publication manager. Thank you, Kayla, for all your help.

I published this collection of poetry, specifically for my posterity—my children, my grandchildren, and my great grandchildren through all time. They all motivate me to reach for the best that is within me; I do not want to disappoint them. They motivate me to improve and try harder each day. I love them so much. I want them all to be happy, to find peace, to appreciate the rough times as well as the good times, and to always remember that they can always look to God for supernal happiness. The processes of life are usually not easy; in fact, they are often long, tedious, tiring, and even painful—and that's okay. Really, it's okay. The schooling that is infused throughout the rough and painful times will absolutely be some of the most important and essential life lessons to understand. Learn them all, and don't back down or skip out because things get tough.

Things are supposed to be hard. Be grateful for all of life's challenges, even for the pain and loss—because all of your difficult experiences, if they are not wasted, can create depth and breadth and passion and vision within you, and eventually, peace and love, understanding and empathy, along with glimpses of true and rare knowledge—all of which, combined together and marinated within the brine of time, will fill you up with joy. I love you all so much. Always believe in your strength and in the intuition that resonates with the spirit that is within you. Respect yourselves. Look to those who respect you, as well as to those whom you respect, for guidance, and always remember to both find and to use the quiet moments of your life to think and to ponder deeply, as well as to go to your Heavenly Father in prayer for His ultimate peace and clarity. He is my kind and caring Father, and he is yours as well. Trust Him. Always trust Him.

I have been a vocal critic of modern technology, but I have been unfair in that thing. I am thankful for the technology that makes writing more practical and publishing possible and reasonable.

I am, of course, most grateful to my Heavenly Father and to His Son for the unquiet mind bequeathed to me and for their continued love for me, despite my rough nature.

For—

Within the Splinters . . .

. . . There is Hope.

Beyond the Splinters . . .

. . . There is Peace.

Yes—

. . . There *is* Peace.